# THE SPY FIVE™
# OPERATION BILLION GAZILLION

by **Spencer Strange**

with *words*

**Andrea Menotti**

and

*pictures* **Kelly Kennedy**

Scholastic Inc.

New York  Toronto  London  Auckland  Sydney
Mexico City  New Delhi  Hong Kong  Buenos Aires

Visit the Spy Five web site at
**www.scholastic.com/spyfive**

Your new password is:

**gazillion** ✏

Use this password
to access a new
game!

ISBN 0-439-70352-2

Copyright © 2004 by Scholastic Inc.

Photo top of p. 7 © Nick Clements/Photodisc Red/Getty Images

Photo bottom of p. 7 © David Buffington/Photodisc Green/Getty Images

12  11  10  9  8  7  6  5  4  3  2  1          5  6  7  8  9/0

Printed in the U.S.A.

First printing, January 2005

# CHAPTERS

# CHAPTER 1
# WE GET GYPPED

One Tuesday morning, Ursula came flying into my homeroom and plopped a newspaper on my desk.

"Look," she said, completely out of breath, pointing to the article on top.

It said:

**Anonymous Donor Gives Books to All City Schools**

"So? What's the big deal?" I asked.

"Read it!" she insisted.

# Anonymous Donor Gives

## *BOOKS ARRIVE BY THE TRUCKLOAD; STUDENTS*

by TRAVIS WESTLEY
STAFF WRITER

Students and teachers across the city celebrated the arrival of truckloads of books, donated to all city schools by a wealthy individual who has chosen to remain unknown.

The books arrived at schools throughout the city Wednesday through Friday last week, greeted by excited students and teachers.

"It was just such a wonderful surprise," said librarian Patricia Gomez at M.S. 2132. "Our library budget gets cut every year, so it gets harder and harder to bring in new and exciting books. But now we have a huge selection—thanks to our mysterious friend!"

"I was getting *real* tired of the books in our library," said seventh-grader Alexis Williams. "Most of them were from, like, back in the 1980s or something."

"Yeah," agreed sixth-grader Leo Serra. "There was nothing I wanted to read, so I just read nothing."

"I read the magazines," added seventh-grader Mina Petrovich. "But that was about it."

Trucks delivered books to city schools all last week.

# Books to All City Schools

## AND TEACHERS CELEBRATE WINDFALL

Students at M.S. 1039 browse through some of their new books.

Principals throughout the city received letters two weeks ago announcing the donation and listing a delivery time.

"The letter had no return address," said Principal Nat Skipper of P.S. 3321. "It just said, 'expect a delivery of books on Wednesday at 4:30.' And sure enough, they arrived. I just looked out my window, and there was a big white truck. There were so many books, we had to buy a whole bunch of new shelves for our library."

Students all over the city helped with unpacking and shelving the books, which included everything from time-honored classics to current best-selling novels for children and young adults.

Deliveries to elementary schools also included hardcover picture books.

"We just want to say thank you to the person who donated all the books," said fourth-grader Sasha Houston. "Because they made our library a lot fuller. And a lot better."

"I wish there was a way we could write thank-you notes to the donor," said librarian Emily Beckerlee of P.S. 1442. "But instead we'll just have to hope that the donor reads this article. So, whoever you are, THANK YOU! Your gift will keep on giving for a long, long time."

P.S. 1442 student Deanna Carter hands a stack of books ready for shelving to librarian Emily Beckerlee.

"Did a truckload of books arrive at *our* school last week?" Ursula asked, after she'd given me about two seconds to read. "I don't *think* so."

"Yeah, *I* didn't hear anything about that," I agreed.

"I was just in the library on Wednesday," Ursula said. "And Miss Butt *definitely* didn't mention any new books."

In case you thought "Miss Butt" was some kind of mean nickname for our school librarian, it's not. That's her actual name. I'm not kidding. You'd think she'd get it legally changed, but she didn't, or at least she hasn't so far. It's really hard to keep a straight face when you say it, so instead most of us try to avoid saying her name at all. Ursula doesn't have any trouble, though.

"What could've happened?" I asked. "It says *all* city schools got books."

"I don't know," Ursula said. "But we've *got* to investigate this one."

"Investigate what?" asked Julian, who walked into the room right then.

"*Look,*" Ursula said, snatching the newspaper from my desk and dropping it on Julian's. "All the schools in this entire city got free books last week from some gazillionaire."

"Did *we* get free books?" Julian asked, looking puzzled.

"Not that I can tell," Ursula said.

"Oooh," Julian said. "No love for M.S. 1024!"

M.S. 1024, OUR SCHOOL

M.S. stands for "Middle School"

All New York City schools have a number

"We *have* to find out what happened," Ursula said. "'Cause if we got left out, that is *so* NOT fair."

## ✳ ✳ ✳ ✳

We brought Blitz and Anika up to speed at lunch.

"Our school never gets the good stuff," Blitz complained. "I know schools where they get basketball players and rap stars to come talk at assemblies. And what do we get? *Nothing.*"

"Are you *sure* we didn't get any books?" Anika asked. "Have you checked with...the library?"

"You mean Miss *Butt*?" Julian asked with a grin.

Blitz cackled.

"You guys are so immature!" Ursula scolded. "It's her *name*. Get over it."

"She should get married and become Mrs. Something Else," Julian said. "ASAP."

"She could just change her name if she wanted to, without getting married," Anika pointed out.

"She could even just change a *letter* of her name and be Miss Burt or something," I suggested.

"She could just be *Miss B*," Blitz said. "A lot of teachers do that when they have names people can't say."

"*Anyway*," Ursula said, turning to Anika, "to answer your question, I was in the library earlier this week, and I didn't see any new books. But I haven't talked to Miss Butt about it yet. I think we should go see her after school."

And then she thought for a second.

"Or maybe just *some* of us should go," she added, eyeing Blitz and Julian.

"HEY!" Blitz protested. "I'm coming!"

"Yeah!" Julian said.

"Fine," Ursula said. "But you better keep a straight face, okay?"

"*But* of course," Blitz grinned.

✳ ✳ ✳ ✳

So we all went to see Miss Butt in the library after school. She was busy re-shelving books when we walked in.

"Miss Butt," Ursula began, "did you hear about that gazillionaire giving truckloads of books to all the schools in this entire city?"

"I did," Miss Butt said. "But for some reason..."

"We got gypped, didn't we?" Blitz interrupted.

"Well, I would have put it another way, but yes, we weren't included in the distribution," she said.

"Do you know why?" Ursula asked.

"I have no idea," Miss Butt said. "I even spoke to Mr. Naulty about it, but he just said there was nothing we could do."

We all fumed at the mention of *that name*.

"As usual, Mr. Naulty could care less if good things happen to us or not!" Anika grumbled.

"Don't worry, we'll get to the bottom of this, Miss Butt," Ursula said firmly.

Julian and Blitz both looked at me when Ursula said that, and I knew exactly what they were thinking. I also knew we weren't gonna make it.

"Excuse us," I said quickly, and the three of us backed out the door. We all burst out laughing as soon as we got into the hall.

A few seconds later, Ursula and Anika were standing in front of us, looking at us with raised eyebrows.

"You *promised* you'd keep a straight face!" Ursula yelled.

"Why'd you have to go and say 'We'll get to the bottom of this, Miss Butt'?" Julian asked. "We were doing fine up till then!"

"Yeah," Blitz said. "That was just *too much*."

Ursula looked at them both with her lips pressed into a thin line. And then she turned to *me*.

"And *you*," she said. "I would think *you* of all people would be more sensitive when someone has a STRANGE name."

"Hey," I protested. "My name is NOTHING like Butt."

"Yeah," everyone agreed.

You have to admit, "Strange" and "Butt" are in two very different leagues.

"*Ugh*," Ursula said. "If you guys can't handle it, then you should stay out of the library till you GROW UP."

"*But* Ursula!" Julian protested with a grin.

Ursula just glared at him.

"Guess there are no 'buts' about it," Blitz said, and he and Julian slapped high five.

Okay, the joke *was* getting a little old.

### ✳ ✳ ✳ ✳

We met the next day at lunch to discuss exactly how we were going to track down our books.

"*I* think Mr. Naulty knows what happened to the books," Ursula said. "I consider him the prime suspect in this case."

"You think he's hiding the books or something?" Blitz asked.

"I wouldn't put it past him," Ursula said.

"What would he want with a truckload of kids' books?" Anika asked.

"He could sell 'em," Julian said, "like to some mafia crook."

"I could totally see that," Blitz agreed.

"Maybe we should do some surveillance on Mr. Naulty," I suggested.

"*Or* we could go *talk* to him about it," Ursula said.

*Yech.* Everyone made a face like they'd just smelled a fart.

"Are you sure that's *necessary?*" Julian asked.

"Don't you think he'll get mad if he thinks we're accusing him of stealing our books?" Blitz asked.

"I'm not saying we should *accuse* him of anything," Ursula said. "I'm just saying we should go talk to him and see what he says. *And* look for signs that he's lying."

"Like *what?*" Julian asked, looking skeptical.

"Like stumbling over words and saying 'um' a lot," Ursula said.

stumbling over words

"Or not making eye contact," added.

"Exactly," Ursula agreed.

"Or blinking a lot," Anika offered.

no eye contact

blinking

"Or scratching his nose!" Blitz said excitedly. "Haven't you heard that?"

All of us looked blank.

"Well, *I've* heard it," Blitz said.

"Are you sure you're not thinking of Pinocchio?" Anika asked.

SKRITCH SCRATCH

nose scratching?

"*Yes*," Blitz said. "Nose-scratching is a sign of lying. I saw it on TV."

"I'll look it up online tonight," Ursula offered.

nose growing like Pinocchio?

At that point, it was time to go back inside for another thrilling afternoon, so we all agreed to meet the next morning in Anika and Blitz's homeroom. We figured it'd be better to talk to Mr. Naulty in the morning, since lately he's been getting kind of ferocious in the afternoon.

# CHAPTER 2
# THE NOSE KNOWS

"Guess what?" Ursula said the next morning when she showed up to meet the rest of us in Anika and Blitz's homeroom. "Blitz was right. See?"

She showed us a printout that had a picture of a guy scratching his nose and the words "Is Your Boyfriend Lying?"

Unfortunately, Blitz wasn't there to say "I told you so." He's been having oversleeping problems again—apparently he's been staying up late working on a bunch of new inventions.

So, after giving Blitz another minute, we went down to Mr. Naulty's office without him. Everyone was pretty quiet—I could tell they were kind of nervous (not that anyone was admitting it, though).

"This should be *interesting*," Anika whispered to me as we headed down the stairs.

Mr. Naulty's secretary, Mrs. Spicer, smiled and said hello to all of us as we walked into the main office. She's pretty nice, kind of like a grandma for the whole school.

"We're here to see Mr. Naulty," Ursula explained in a hushed voice, pointing at Mr. Naulty's closed office door in the back.

"You *are?*" Mrs. Spicer asked, looking surprised. "Did you make an *appointment?*"

Mrs. Spicer pointed to Mr. Naulty's appointment calendar, which definitely didn't have an appointment marked in it for us. Why do people ask questions when they already know the answers?

"Sorry, no, we didn't make an appointment," Ursula said. "Should we come back another time?"

"Well, maybe Mr. Naulty can squeeze you in," Mrs. Spicer said with a smile. "Why don't you have a seat on the couch. He just stepped out to pick up his morning muffin. He should be back shortly."

So we all sat on the couch and waited.

"Trail mix?" Mrs. Spicer offered, holding out a clear plastic bag full of nuts and raisins.

"No thanks," we all said.

I had no appetite at all, and definitely not for that bird-foody stuff.

After about a minute of Mrs. Spicer crunching on her trail mix and talking about the rainy weather, Mr. Naulty showed up carrying a giant blueberry muffin. Or *half* of a giant blueberry muffin, I should say.

He was definitely surprised to see us sitting there waiting for him.

"What are *they* doing here?" he asked Mrs. Spicer, as if we weren't within hearing range.

"I don't know, actually," she said cheerfully, turning to us. "What *are* you here for?"

"We're here because of *this*," Ursula said, standing up to show her newspaper article to Mr. Naulty.

Mr. Naulty looked quickly at the article.

"How come *we* didn't get any books?" Anika asked.

"I don't know," Mr. Naulty said gruffly. "I guess they must've missed us. Too bad."

I looked at the others to see if they'd noticed that Mr. Naulty did NOT make eye contact with any of us when he said that. Anika gave me a little nod to show that she was thinking the same thing.

no eye contact

GUESS THEY MUST'VE MISSED US. TOO BAD.

PRINCIPAL

"It says here that principals got letters from the donor," Ursula said. "Didn't you get a letter?"

"I never saw *any* letter about *any* books," Mr. Naulty insisted. "Like I said, there must've been an oversight."

"But can't we *do* something about it?" Ursula asked. "Can't we *call* somebody?"

"We don't know who the donor is," Mr. Naulty said. "That's what *anonymous* means."

"We *know* what anonymous means," Ursula said, with a little too much emphasis on the "know." We all winced.

"Well, then you *know* there's no one we can call," Mr. Naulty said, giving his "know" plenty of umph, too.

"But it's not *fair* that everyone else got new books and we didn't!" Ursula protested.

"Students in this school don't respect books anyway," Mr. Naulty said. "All our books just get beat up and torn apart."

"Not *everyone* treats books that way," Ursula said with a frown.

"I think people would be *very* respectful if the books were new," Anika said. "Especially if the books were a special gift."

"Can't we *try* to see if we can get our books somehow?" I asked. "Can't you talk to other principals, or check your mail again, or *something?*"

And that's when Mr. Naulty did it...

# HE SCRATCHED HIS NOSE!

It was really quick, but he definitely did it!

"I'm sorry," he said. "But there's nothing I can do about it."

And with that, he turned, walked into his office, and closed the door.

"I'm sorry, too," Mrs. Spicer said, making a sad face. "It's like Santa Claus forgot about us, isn't it?"

We all gave Mrs. Spicer weak smiles and headed out. Mrs. Spicer is really nice and all, but she always seems to be under the impression that we're still in kindergarten.

$$* \quad * \quad * \quad *$$

We told Blitz the whole story that day at lunch, including the part about the nose-scratching.

"I can't *believe* I missed it!" Blitz complained.

"He's lying about something," Ursula said. "No doubt about it."

"You know what I think?" Julian said.

"That Mr. Naulty's hiding the books in the basement?" Ursula asked.

"Yeah," Julian said, looking surprised. "How'd you know?"

"It's the most logical hiding place in the whole school," Ursula said. "That storage room could hide a lot."

"Makes sense," I agreed.

The storage room is down the hall from the cafeteria. The janitors store their cleaning supplies in there, so they sometimes leave the door open after school.

I peeked inside once and saw lots of stacked-up chairs and desks, and piles of random stuff covered in sheets. It was creepy, to say the least. Definitely a good hiding place for twenty boxes of books.

"*I* think we should infiltrate," Ursula said.

"Should be pretty easy," I said. "I've seen the door propped open lots of times after school."

"Let's do it today!" Julian said excitedly.

"But we need flashlights and a camera," Blitz protested. "I don't have any of that stuff here today."

"*And* I have my clarinet lesson today," Ursula said. "Tomorrow, okay?"

"Let's do it at 2:30 so I can come, too," Anika said. "'Cause I'm outta here at 3:00 tomorrow, as usual."

And so it was a plan.

# CHAPTER 3
# ROCK, SCISSORS, POWER CHISEL

The next day at 2:30, the five of us met in the stairwell, all geared up and ready to go.

camera

flashlight

"We better hope the door's open," Ursula said.

"If it's not, we still have options," I said.

"Like what?" Blitz asked.

"Well, my Spanish teacher has a bunch of broken chairs in her room," I said. "We could offer to bring her new ones from the storage room."

"And get stuck hauling chairs up four flights of steps?" Ursula shot back.

"Well, at least a janitor would unlock the storage room for us for a reason like that," I said. "And chairs aren't *that* heavy."

"True," Anika said.

So we headed down the steps. When we got to the basement, we peeked out of the stairwell to make sure the coast was clear. No one seemed to be around, so we made our way down the hall to the corner, where we'd be able to see if the storage room door was open.

We peeked around the corner, and fortunately, the door *was* open.

Phew! At least I wasn't going to have to listen to Ursula complain about hauling chairs.

"Let's go!" Blitz said excitedly.

"Wait a second," Julian said. "Shouldn't one of us stay here to warn us if somebody's coming?"

"Good idea," I said.

"It's not gonna be *me*," Blitz said. "I did that job *last* time."

It was true—when we infiltrated the kitchen a while back (to investigate the chicken nuggets), Blitz had been the one to stand guard.

"Maybe it should be the person who caused *problems* last time," Ursula said, eyeing Julian.

"You mean *you*?" Julian asked, glaring at Ursula.

I quickly jumped in before *that* conversation could go any further. When we infiltrated the kitchen, Julian and Ursula had MAJOR problems getting along.

"Let's just do 'rock, paper, scissors,'" I said. "Blitz can sit out, since he was the guard last time. The four of us can do two rounds, and the loser stands guard."

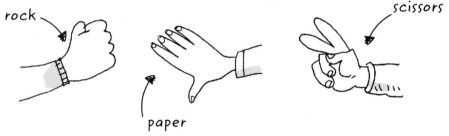

rock

scissors

paper

Everyone nodded...except Ursula.

"I don't believe in 'rock, paper, scissors,'" she said.

"*What*, is it against your religion?" Julian asked in an annoyed voice.

"No," Ursula scowled. "I just don't think the rules work."

"What's wrong with the rules? Rock breaks scissors, scissors cut paper, and paper wraps around rock. Simple!" Blitz said.

"But if you wrap the paper around the rock, eventually the paper will wither away, and the rock will still be there forever," Ursula said.

"Oh *please*," Julian said.

"Or, if the rock can break the scissors, then the rock can *definitely* break the paper. You could just hold up the paper and toss the rock through it," Ursula said.

rock breaks paper

RRRIP!

She *did* have a point there.

"Can't you just accept the rules for now, just this once, since we're kinda in a hurry?" Anika asked.

"Well, we *could* do the version I made up with my sister," Ursula said. "'Rock, scissors, power chisel.'"

**"POWER CHISEL?"** we all said.

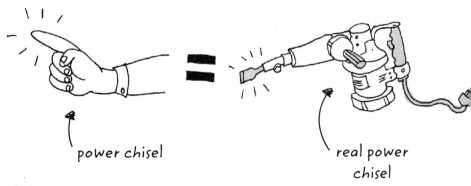

power chisel

real power chisel

"Yeah. The rock breaks the scissors, the power chisel carves the rock, and the scissors cut the power chisel's cord," Ursula explained.

"**FINE!**" we all said.

So, after two rounds of 'rock, scissors, power chisel,' Ursula lost. She actually lost to *me*, on power chisel versus scissors. She was *not* pleased, but she accepted it.

"Make sure to check the *whole* room, okay?" Ursula said as we walked off.

"No, we're just gonna check *half* of it," Julian said, rolling his eyes.

So we headed down the hall to the storage room.

Inside, it was dark and super musty. I groped around for the light switches, but I could only find one set that lit up the front part of the room. And even *that* part was still really dim, so it was good that we had our flashlights.

We spread out and looked around the place, but we didn't see any boxes of books.

Then, suddenly, we heard Ursula calling to us from the doorway.

"Guys! Someone's coming!" she whispered as loudly as possible. "Quick!"

So we dashed to the door, flicked off the lights, tucked away our flashlights, and started walking down the hall, trying to look as innocent as possible.

"Did you find anything?" Ursula whispered to me.

"No," I said.

"Did you search the *whole* room?" she asked.

"We searched as much as we could in three *minutes*," I said, trying to cut the conversation short because I could hear *someone* was getting very close.

And that's when the person turned the corner:

# KELVIN!

Kelvin is one of the janitors at our school—we got to know him when we infiltrated the kitchen, and since then he's always been really nice to us (he likes to call us things like "the undercover bunch" and "the private spies").

A huge smile spread across Kelvin's face when he saw us.

"It's the secret investigators!" he boomed from all the way down the hall. "What are *you* doing here? Are you about to crack another case?"

And that's when I realized that Kelvin could be a real help.

"I think we should tell him," I whispered to the others. "I bet he'd help us out."

"Yeah," the others nodded.

It's THE SECRET INVESTIGATORS!

Kelvin

So when Kelvin got closer, we filled him in.

"We're trying to find out what happened to a big delivery of books we were supposed to get last week," I explained.

"A big delivery of books?" Kelvin repeated. "I never heard anything about that."

"All city schools were supposed to get a big truckload of books that some gazillionaire donated," Ursula explained. "But ours never came."

"How strange!" Kelvin said.

"Or maybe the delivery *came* and Mr. Naulty hid the books somewhere," Julian suggested.

"You think Mr. Naulty's at it again, eh?" Kelvin asked. "I have to admit, I haven't trusted him since you kids caught him helping himself to the chocolate pudding."

"Neither have we," Ursula said grimly.

"We were thinking maybe he hid the books in the storage room," Anika said.

"I keep that storage room pretty organized," Kelvin said, "so I'd know if anything new arrived. But let's check."

And so we went through the storage room a second time, but *again*, we didn't find any books.

"I know all the closets and storage areas in this school, and I haven't seen any new boxes in any of them," Kelvin assured us. "But I'll keep an eye out for you."

"Thanks, Kelvin," we all said, and we headed back upstairs.

"Sounds like the books really *didn't* come," I said as we piled up the stairs.

"I *still* think Mr. Naulty's involved in this somehow," Ursula said. "We just have to figure out *how*."

"Maybe we need to do some surveillance," I suggested.

"I'll work on a new plan of attack over the weekend," Ursula offered.

Everyone else said they'd think about it, too.

"Oh, and you know what I was thinking just now while I was standing guard?" Ursula added.

"What?" Anika asked.

"'Rock, scissors, power chisel' doesn't work either," Ursula said. "If the power chisel can cut the *rock*, then it can cut the *scissors*, too."

"But not if the scissors cut the power cord," I reminded her.

"It would depend on which one acted first," Ursula said. "So there's not a clear-cut winner. Then there's *also* a problem with the rock versus the power chisel. If the rock can smash the scissors, then technically it could smash the power chisel, too."

"Gimme a *break*," Julian said. "You're *crazy*."

"I want a perfect system," Ursula said. "So I guess it's back to the drawing board. I'll keep you posted."

# CHAPTER 4
# CLUE CITY

On Monday morning, Ursula came running into my homeroom with a newspaper *again*. This time Julian was already there with me.

"Look!" she said.

"*Another* article?" I asked.

"No, it's the same one," she said, dropping the article on my desk and pulling a magnifying glass out of her pocket. "But look what we can see."

And I looked through the magnifying glass and saw, very clearly, on the side of the truck:

## BARNSDALE DELIVERY COMPANY

"I looked up the company online, and I found their phone number," Ursula said, showing us a printout. "We can call and let them know we never got our delivery, and then they can contact the gazillionaire, and he can send out another truck for us!"

Ursula was *totally* out of breath when she got done saying that.

"Good plan!" I said.

Even Julian seemed impressed.

"Lemme see!" he said, reaching for the magnifying glass.

newspaper
article

Just as Ursula was catching her breath, Anika and Blitz came tearing in with another cool clue.

"Look!" Anika said, waving an envelope. "This is an actual letter from the gazillionaire!"

We all gasped and went running up to see the letter.

"I got it at my old elementary school," Anika explained. "My little brother goes there now, so when my older brother and I went there to pick him up last Friday after school, I stopped in to see the principal. She still remembers me, so she was really nice about it. She even said I could keep the letter."

"Sweet!" Julian said.

"See the postmark?" Anika said. "I checked online, and that zip code covers this area."

She showed us a map she'd printed out from the internet.

"Of course, anyone can mail a letter from anywhere," Anika pointed out. "But I think it's pretty safe to say that the gazillionaire lives or works in this neighborhood."

gazillionaire's zip code

NEW YORK NY 10017
PM

Principal
P.S. 1132
200 West 11⬚⬚⬚eet
New Y⬚

W 50th St
W 49th St
W 48th St
W 47th St
W 46th St
W 45th St
W 44th St
W 43rd St
W 42nd St

Madison Ave
Park Ave

Avenue Of The Americas

W 45th St

7th Ave

E 44th St
E 43rd St
E 42nd St

E 45th St

Bryant Park

5th Ave

Broadway

map of the
gazillionaire's
neighborhood

W 38th St
W 37th St
W 36th St
W 35th St
W 34th St
W 33rd St
W 32nd St

Madison Ave

Park Ave Tunnel

E 41st St
E 40th St
E 39th St
E 38th St

E 33rd St

Park Ave S

Lexington Ave

3rd Ave

E 31st St
E 30th St
E 29th St

letter from
gazillionaire

Dear Principal,

An anonymous donor is giving twenty
boxes of books (approximately 800 books)
to every New York City school. You'll
find your school's delivery time on the
attached page.

All deliveries are scheduled during
normal opening hours for school buildings.
Please make sure to alert your custodial
staff of the delivery, and please have
a secure area set aside to store the
boxes (which will be carried inside by
the delivery company).

Thank you.

"Nice work!" I said.

"And look what *I* found," Ursula said, showing Anika and Blitz her discovery in the photo and filling them in on the plan.

"Oooh," Anika said. "Looks like we are hot on the trail of Mister Billion Gazillion!"

And then she thought for a second.

"Or *Miz* Billion Gazillion, of course."

✳ ✳ ✳ ✳

After school that day, we all met at the pay phone downstairs to call the Barnsdale Delivery Company. We decided Anika would do the talking, since she's the best at being polite on the phone.

So we dialed the number and turned the volume up so we could all hear. The phone rang about five times before anybody picked up.

"Barnsdale Deliveries," a man's voice said. "This is Phil."

Phil sounded like he was totally wiped out.

"Um, yes, hello," Anika began. "I'm calling about the book deliveries to New York City schools?"

"Those deliveries are all done," Phil said gruffly.

"But our school didn't receive any books," Anika said.

"Sorry—can't help ya," Phil said. "All deliveries are complete. Last I heard from the client was last Friday, and he was asking me to mail him the invoice. That means there's nothing left to deliver."

"Is there any way we can get in touch with the client?" Anika asked.

"Nope," Phil said. "The client doesn't want anyone to know who he is. He wouldn't even give me his phone number."

COULD YOU POSSIBLY PASS ALONG A MESSAGE FOR US?

"Could you possibly pass along a message for us?" Anika asked.

"Sorry," Phil said. "I already mailed out the invoice today, or I could've stuck in a note for you."

"Could you write to him again?" Anika asked. "*Please?*"

I could tell Anika was really pressing her luck.

"Listen, I'd really like to help—you sound like a nice kid," Phil said. "But I'm *very* busy here."

"Maybe someone *else* could help us?" Anika asked.

I winced, because I knew Anika was really *really* pressing her luck now.

"*I'm* the only one who handles this account," Phil said. "And besides, everyone else here is just as busy as me. Sorry we can't help. Have a good day."

"Well, thank—" Anika started to say, but the phone went CLICK. Anika sighed and hung up.

"I *tried*," she said. "But he just wouldn't give an inch."

"Well, at least we found out the gazillionaire's a *man*," Ursula pointed out. "Remember Phil said the client wouldn't give *his* phone number, and that he'd mailed *him* an invoice."

"If only we could get Phil to cough up that *address*," Julian said.

"I think we should have Miss Butt call Phil back tomorrow," Ursula said. "Maybe he'll help if *she* asks him, since she's an adult."

"It's so annoying when *some people* think they can blow off other people just 'cause of their *age*," Anika complained, rolling her eyes.

"It's called *ageism*," Ursula said, shaking her head. "There are *tons* of ageists in this world. Bunch of turkeys if you ask me."

"*I* think we should fight back," Blitz said suddenly. "And I have the *perfect* weapon. Come to my place after school tomorrow and I'll show you."

The next day, we went over to Blitz's place after school—everyone but Anika, because she had to go home at 3:00 like usual.

Blitz's room was messier than I'd ever seen it. It was almost like we were wading in a flood of clothes.

"Hold on," Blitz said, grabbing armloads of clothes and dumping them into the closet. "Lemme get this stuff out of the way."

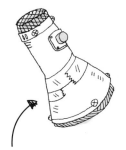

voice changer

Julian went right over to Blitz's workbench and looked at the stuff on it.

"What's this?" Julian asked, holding up a little tube-shaped device.

"That," Blitz said, dumping a load of clothes on his bed, "is a voice changer."

"**A WHAT?**" Julian asked immediately. "Lemme try!"

"Just press the button and talk into it," Blitz said. "It's all set to go."

So Julian pressed the button and talked. His voice came out all deep and low, like some tough guy.

"Cool!" Julian said.

Of course, Ursula and I had to try it, too. Our voices all came out just like Julian's.

"You made this thing?" I asked.

"Just finished," Blitz nodded. "It's one of the projects I've been working on these past couple weeks."

"How'd you do it?" Julian asked.

"I ordered the chip from an electronics catalog and rigged it up with a speaker and microphone," Blitz explained. "I didn't think it'd come in handy so fast!"

"You mean *this* is the device you want to use on Phil?" Ursula asked.

"Exactly," Blitz said. "If we call Phil with it, we could make him think we were a teacher or even a *principal*. Then maybe he'd be willing to lift a finger for us."

"Oooh," Julian said. "I like it."

"It sounds a little electronic," Ursula said. "Don't you think he'd know it was a fake voice?"

"I think we could pull it off," Blitz said, thinking for a second. "If we called him from a speaker phone, we could say the phone wasn't working right or something—like it was making voices sound funny."

"Good call," I said.

"Let's try it!" Julian said. "If it doesn't work, we can just hang up, no big deal."

"There's a speaker phone in the kitchen," Blitz said. "Let's go!"

So we all ran to Blitz's kitchen and stood around the phone while Ursula dialed the number she'd found. They'd appointed *me* to do the talking for some reason, so I stood there with the voice changer at the ready.

Again, the phone rang lots of times before anyone picked it up. This time it was a *woman's* voice.

"Barnsdale Deliveries," she said. "This is Kathleen."

I took a deep breath and started to speak.

"Hi Kathleen," I said, using her name since I thought that sounded adult-like. "I'm calling about the school book deliveries. Is Phil there?"

There was a long pause. We all practically stopped breathing. Was Kathleen thinking the voice sounded fake, or was she buying it?

"Is this...Mr. Alexander?" Kathleen asked.

I looked at the others with wide eyes. Who was Mr. Alexander? And what did he have to do with the book deliveries? I decided to see if I could get her to say a little more.

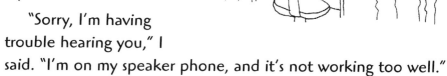

"Sorry, I'm having trouble hearing you," I said. "I'm on my speaker phone, and it's not working too well."

"I can tell," Kathleen said. "Your voice sounds a little funny on my end, too."

"Is Phil there?" I repeated.

"Phil's not here right now," Kathleen said. "But he told me you might call to check on the invoice."

## THE INVOICE?!

Everyone's jaw dropped open. Did Kathleen think I was the gazillionaire himself? Was the gazillionaire's name Mr. Alexander?

I decided to keep playing along, since I knew a little about the invoice from what Phil had said the day before.

"Was the invoice sent out yesterday?" I asked.

"Yes, sir, just like you asked," Kathleen answered.

It was really funny to have someone call me "sir," and especially to have her think I was some big-shot gazillionaire! I was getting bolder and bolder by the second...so I decided to really go for it.

"And you're sure you got the right address?" I asked.

"The address?" Kathleen asked. "Let me check the files."

Ursula, Julian, and Blitz looked at me with huge eyes and hanging-open mouths as we waited for Kathleen to come back. Ursula had her notebook at the ready so she could write everything down.

"565 Fifth Avenue," Kathleen said when she returned.

"10017?" I asked, figuring it would sound good to throw in the zip code, since we already knew it, thanks to Anika.

"10017," Kathleen confirmed.

"Great," I said. "Thanks for your help."

"Sure thing," Kathleen said.

And we both hung up. I could hardly believe what I'd just done!

"SCORE!" Julian cheered.

"Awesome!" Blitz chimed in.

"You're amazing!" Ursula gushed.

It was weird to hear those words come out of *Ursula's* mouth!

"I *knew* this thing would come in handy!" Blitz said, talking into the voice changer. "Perfect for impersonating a gazillionaire!"

But before we could finish celebrating, we heard...

## "NATHAN BLITZER!"

We all turned to see Blitz's mom looking *very* serious.

"Where did you get that voice?" Mrs. Blitzer asked.

"When did *you* get home?" Blitz asked in his normal voice.

"Just now," Mrs. Blitzer said, holding out her hand. "Give me that...thing."

"It's a voice changer," Blitz said. "I built it last—"

"Please give it to me now," Mrs. Blitzer interrupted.

And so Blitz sighed and handed it over.

Mrs. Blitzer

"Are you using this to make prank calls?" Mrs. Blitzer demanded, looking at the voice changer with a frown.

"No," Blitz said.

"Then why are you all standing around the phone?" she asked.

"Um, well...it's hard to explain," Blitz said.

"Well, I'm afraid this is going to have to go in the *cabinet*," Mrs. Blitzer said.

"BUT MOM!" Blitz said. "I just finished building it!"

"Tough," she said. "I do NOT want you impersonating adults on the phone. It's *inappropriate*."

Blitz tried to protest some more, but it was hopeless. Mrs. Blitzer told us all it was time for us to go, and then marched off down the hall with the voice changer in hand. Blitz walked us to the door looking very depressed.

"Are you gonna get it back?" Julian asked.

"Probably not," Blitz said with a sigh. "She's locking it in her file cabinet. The last time something got locked up in there I never saw it again. I call it 'the black hole.'"

"Can't you negotiate?" Ursula asked.

"Not with *her*," Blitz said, shaking his head. "I'll just build another one next week. A *better* one."

And with that, Julian, Ursula, and I said our good-byes and walked down the stairs quietly. Ursula was the first person to get back in a happy mood.

"Well," she said. "Look on the bright side. We're *this* close to getting our books now!"

That was true—at least the voice changer didn't die for nothing.

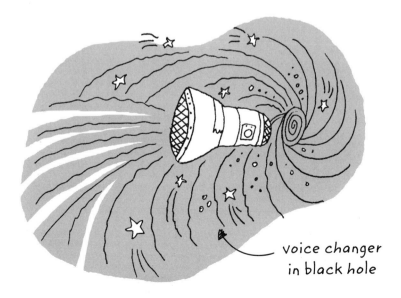

voice changer
in black hole

# CHAPTER 6
# PSSSST!

he next morning before school, Ursula came to visit me and Julian in homeroom. She had a letter to Mr. Alexander all typed up and ready to go.

"I already stopped by the library and showed it to Miss Butt," Ursula said. "She was *really* amazed that we got the delivery company to spill the beans. She said she'd definitely help us. I figured we should have the gazillionaire talk to *her* to set up the delivery, not Mr. Naulty."

"Good idea," I said.

"*And* I think we should deliver the letter in person so Mr. Alexander gets it right away," Ursula added, watching proudly as Julian and I read the letter.

It sounded all fancy and frilly, like *somebody* used a thesaurus.

Mr. Alexander
565 Fifth Avenue
New York, NY 10017

Dear Mr. Alexander,

　　We were very excited to hear about your
enormously generous donation to the schools
of New York City. However, unfortunately, our
school, M.S. 1024, did not receive a book
delivery like the other schools. We don't know
why this occurred, but we'd be tremendously
grateful if you could send a truck full of books
to our school, too. Our school has lots of
dilapidated books and not very many decent ones.

　　To contact our school, please use the phone
number on the next page, and please ask to speak
with our librarian, Miss Butt. The next page also
has a map of our school's location in case the
truck got lost last time.

　　Thank you for taking the time to read our
letter.


Sincerely,


*Ursula Park*

Ursula Park                    Anika Marshall



Spencer Strange                Nathan Blitzer



　　　　　　Julian Garcia

"Sign above your name," Ursula said proudly, handing me a pen, "in nice handwriting."

"Why is MY name last?" Julian wanted to know.

"Does it really matter?" Ursula asked.

"You *know* you put my name last on purpose," Julian said. "Admit it."

Just when I thought we were headed for another Julian-Ursula showdown, I heard a noise coming from the doorway:

# "PSSSST!"

We all looked up to see, of all people, *Mrs. Spicer* standing there. She motioned for us to come over.

"I saw you walking in," Mrs. Spicer said to Ursula, "so I thought I'd come tell you what I discovered yesterday..."

And Mrs. Spicer's voice lowered to a whisper...

"*...about the book delivery.*"

"What?" Ursula asked, her eyes wide.

"Before I say anything, let me just say that I'm only telling you this because I know how much it means to you," Mrs. Spicer said, still whispering. "And I think it's important that you know the truth. Mr. Naulty would not be pleased if he knew I'd told you, of course. It's just so *unfortunate*...I feel very badly about it."

"What happened?" I asked, hoping Mrs. Spicer would hurry up and get to the point.

"Well, I was helping Mr. Naulty with his mail yesterday—sometimes his mail can really pile up, you know," Mrs. Spicer said. "And I found a letter that said we were supposed to have a book delivery at 4:45 on Thursday the tenth."

We all gasped.

"So why didn't we get the books?" Ursula asked.

"Well, it appears that the truck came and the driver found no one here to receive the delivery," Mrs. Spicer said. "Mr. Naulty rarely stays beyond 4:30, you see. The custodian and janitors are here till late in the evening, but the doors are always locked, and if they're not expecting a delivery, they won't open the doors for anyone."

"So where did our books go?" I asked.

"Well, *then* Mr. Naulty got a *second* letter last Monday saying that he could contact a certain delivery company any day last week to schedule a new delivery time," she continued. "But the letter said that if they didn't hear from him by the end of the week, they would..."

She winced.

"They'd *what?*" Ursula asked impatiently.

"Return the books to the warehouse," Mrs. Spicer finished.

We all gasped.

"We *told* Mr. Naulty about this last week!" Ursula said. "If he cared, he could've checked his mail and called!"

"He just doesn't care if anything good ever happens to us!" Julian said.

"I'm sorry," Mrs. Spicer said. "He's just very...busy."

"The *other* principals weren't too busy to make sure they got books for *their* students," Ursula said flatly.

"I know, it's very disappointing," Mrs. Spicer agreed, making her sad face again. "It upsets me very much."

"We're not giving up yet," Ursula said. "We found out the donor's name and address, and we're going to try to arrange another delivery."

"Really?" Mrs. Spicer said, looking amazed. "You managed all that?"

"Yup," Ursula said.

"What movers and shakers you are!" Mrs. Spicer gushed. "I'm so *impressed*!"

It looked like Mrs. Spicer was ready to grab all of us into a big group hug.

"Thanks," we all said, backing away ever so slightly.

"Well, if there's any way I can help, just let me know," Mrs. Spicer said.

WHAT MOVERS AND SHAKERS YOU ARE!

"There *is*, actually," Ursula said. "If the donor calls, he'll be calling the school's main phone number, since the library doesn't have an outside line. So if someone named Mr. Alexander calls, he should talk to Miss Butt down in the library. She said she'd handle all the arrangements."

"I will certainly make sure the call gets through," Mrs. Spicer promised, and then she stopped and thought for a second. "What was the name again?"

"Mr. Alexander," Ursula said. "Like Alexander the Great."

"Perfect. I'll remember that!" Mrs. Spicer said excitedly. "I hope he calls! It'd be so wonderful to see that library full of nice new books for you children to read!"

"That's what we're going to make happen," Ursula said firmly.

✳ ✳ ✳ ✳

After we talked with Mrs. Spicer, we all ran to Anika and Blitz's homeroom to fill them in. Blitz was already there, and he'd already told Anika about the call to the delivery company (and about us getting busted by his mom). They were both shocked to hear the news from Mrs. Spicer.

"So *that's* what Mr. Naulty was lying about," Anika said with one eyebrow raised. "He knew he hadn't checked his mail, but he just didn't care enough to bother."

"Typical," Blitz said.

"Today after school we're going to deliver this letter to Mr. Alexander's building," Ursula said, handing the letter to Anika. "There's a space for you both to sign."

"Cool," Anika said, looking at the letter. "*Man*, Julian, do you think you signed your name big enough?"

"He was getting back at me for putting his name last," Ursula glowered.

"Which you did on purpose," Julian added.

"Okay, let's *not* go there," Anika said, quickly signing her name with her purple ink pen. "So you're actually planning to give this to the gazillionaire *in person*?"

"We figure his building'll have a front desk, and we can just leave it there," Ursula said. "He probably has important meetings all day long. We wouldn't want to bug him or anything."

"If he's that busy and important, how do we know he'll read our letter?" Anika asked as she passed the letter to Blitz.

"Yeah," Blitz agreed. "What if it just gets buried under all his other mail?"

We all thought about that one for a moment.

"I know *just* the thing," Anika suddenly said. "I'll work on it this morning and show you after lunch."

✳ ✳ ✳ ✳

After lunch, Anika arrived with her creation:

Anika's masterpiece

MR. ALEXANDER
565 FIFTH AVENUE
NEW YORK, NY 10017

It was an envelope—the biggest, brightest, most girly envelope I'd ever seen. It was covered in flowers, swirls, and zigzags in every color of the rainbow. You could tell she was really proud of it.

"I got the paper and markers from Miss Manning and worked on it all through lunch," Anika explained. "It really says 'open me,' don't you think?"

"It definitely says *something*," Julian said, looking at Anika's creation with raised eyebrows.

"If we put the letter in this envelope, there's no way Mr. Gazillion will miss it," Anika said. "That's the point."

"Good idea," Ursula said. "I like it."

"I just wish I could come with you guys," Anika said. "But I know my brother's gonna want to go straight home like usual."

"Aren't you *ever* allowed to go home by yourself?" Ursula asked.

"My parents are really overprotective," Anika groaned. "But I'm working on them. Little by little."

"I can't come either," Blitz said sadly. "I'm grounded for impersonating."

"Oh, sorry," I said with a wince.

"It's no big deal," Blitz shrugged. "I'll just use the time to work on more gadgets."

And so it was settled: It would be me, Julian, and Ursula heading down to Mr. Alexander's building that day after school to deliver the girliest envelope the world had ever seen.

# CHAPTER 7

# OPERATION GIRLY ENVELOPE

J ulian, Ursula, and I set out for Fifth Avenue right after Homework Club. We had to take the subway downtown and then walk a couple of blocks across town. It was 4:15 by the time we finally got there.

Mr. Alexander's building

With Ursula holding the envelope, we went inside and walked up to the front desk.

"We have a delivery for Mr. Alexander," Ursula said proudly, handing the envelope to the man at the front desk.

The man set down his jelly donut, licked his fingers, and picked up our envelope.

"Mr. Alexander?" the man asked. "Do you know what floor he's on?"

"Um, no," Ursula said. "You've never heard of him?"

"Lots of people work in this building, sweetheart," the man said. "I'll look him up."

Ursula turned to me and Julian with a puzzled look as we waited for Mr. Jelly Donut to type Mr. Alexander's name into his computer. I know exactly what Ursula was thinking—why hadn't this guy ever heard of a big shot like Mr. Alexander?

"Maybe gazillionaires are a dime a dozen in this building," Ursula whispered.

It *was* a pretty fancy building.

"Here we are—Jonathan Alexander, 24th floor," Jelly said, picking up the phone. "I'll give him a call."

We all looked at each other with huge eyes as Jelly dialed—Mr. Alexander was being bothered on our account? Would he be mad?

"Mr. Alexander," Jelly began, "there's a real pretty envelope here for you. Delivered by a bunch of kids."

I suddenly felt a huge wave of embarrassment. I imagined Mr. Alexander up in his enormous office, realizing that there was only one reason why a bunch of kids would be delivering him a "real pretty envelope." Was he annoyed that we'd figured him out? Or was he *impressed*? Or maybe just surprised? And what did he look like, anyway? It was tough to imagine him with nothing to go on.

Jelly was off the phone really fast.

"He said he'd pick it up on his way out," Jelly explained, grabbing his donut again. "I'll make sure he gets it."

"Thank you," Ursula said in a very dignified way.

And we turned to go.

"I wonder what time Mr. Alexander leaves for the day," Ursula said as we headed outside.

I looked at my watch. It was 4:25.

"Probably not before 5:00," I said. "And if he's like my mom, not before 7:30."

"Do you guys want to wait a little while and see if he comes out? We could sit over there," Ursula suggested, pointing to a bench across the street that had a view of Mr. Alexander's lobby. "We'd know which one was Mr. Alexander because we'd see him pick up the envelope."

"We won't be able to see *anything* from way over there," Julian argued.

"Are you kidding? Our envelope's so huge, we'd be able to see it from the *moon*," Ursula insisted. "I think we should at least wait a *little* while."

"I have to get home," Julian said. "Sorry."

I could tell Julian didn't want Ursula to know the *reason* he had to get home—his grandma and her 5:00-or-else rule.

"Can *you* stay, Spencer?" Ursula asked. "Just for, like, half an hour?"

I really didn't think we had much chance of seeing the gazillionaire come out anytime soon—I figure you don't get to be a gazillionaire unless you work pretty late. But then I thought of Ursula sitting on the bench by herself and felt bad leaving her alone.

"I can stick around for half an hour," I said with a shrug.

So Julian left, and Ursula and I went over to the bench and sat down.

It was kind of cold. And windy. Not exactly sit-on-a-bench-outside weather.

"Do you want a Fig Newton?" Ursula asked, pulling a bag of cookies out of her backpack. They looked kind of smushed.

"No thanks," I said.

"Why not? Do you have something against figs?" Ursula asked.

"I'm just not hungry," I explained.

I could tell this was going to be a loooooong half an hour. I pulled out my notebook and a pencil so I could draw.

"Don't draw *me*," Ursula said. "You always draw me ugly."

"I do *not*," I said.

"Please don't tell me that's how you think I really look," Ursula said, rolling her eyes.

"Why do you care so much?" I asked. "Why does it matter how I draw you?"

"It matters because everyone *else* looks better," Ursula said, looking all pouty.

Since we had some waiting time ahead of us, I decided I'd try drawing Ursula in a *different* way, just to see what she'd say. She sat there eating her Fig Newtons and watching the lobby across the street while I drew.

She didn't exactly appreciate my masterpiece (ha ha).

Ursula as beauty queen

So anyway, eventually it got to be 5:00, and we still hadn't seen anyone pick up the girly envelope from Mr. Jelly Donut. It was starting to get a little dark, too, so it wasn't so easy to see all the way across the street anymore.

"You think we should move in closer?" I asked.

"What if we missed him while you were *bothering* me with your drawing?" Ursula fretted, looking at me with a scowl.

"He wouldn't have come out before five," I said. "You don't get to be a gazillionaire by sneaking out before—"

But I didn't have a chance to say "the five o'clock whistle" because Ursula screamed...

And sure enough, I looked up to see a man coming out of the building with the girly envelope in hand.

So there was the actual Mr. Alexander. Funny, he didn't look like I thought he would. I guess I was expecting someone in a fancy suit. With a nice briefcase. And maybe he'd hop into a stretch limo or something. But Mr. Alexander just walked off down the street, carrying the girly envelope under his arm.

"Let's follow him!" Ursula said.

I nodded, quickly grabbing my backpack and slinging it over my shoulder. I have to admit, I was very curious about this gazillionaire guy.

# CHAPTER 8

# FOLLOW THAT GAZILLIONAIRE

**U**rsula and I followed Mr. Alexander as he walked a couple of blocks north on Fifth Avenue, then turned right on 49th Street and started heading east.

"He walks a long way for a rich dude," Ursula said. "Shouldn't he have a chauffeur or something?"

"Maybe he likes the exercise," I said with a shrug.

Things definitely got a *lot* stranger after that:

5:10: Mr. A goes down into subway.

Note: Plenty of taxis around, but he picks the subway?

51ST ST STATION UPTOWN 6

HE GIVES AWAY TRUCKLOADS OF BOOKS, BUT HE CAN'T AFFORD A CAB?

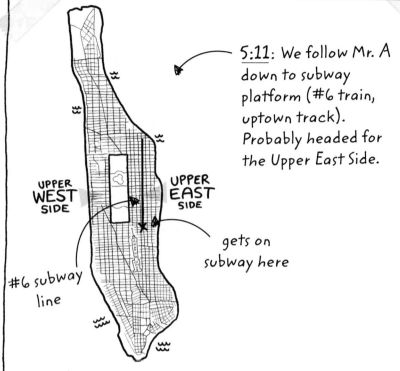

**5:11:** We follow Mr. A down to subway platform (#6 train, uptown track). Probably headed for the Upper East Side.

UPPER **WEST** SIDE

UPPER **EAST** SIDE

gets on subway here

#6 subway line

**5:12:** While waiting for subway, Mr. A sits on bench and opens our letter. Reads...and smiles! Ursula very happy. About ready to burst with joy.

HE LIKES IT!

5:16: Train arrives. Mr. A gets onboard. So do we. Very crowded.

5:30: Mr. A gets off at 86th Street and then walks a couple blocks to his apartment building. Nice place, lobby like a hotel. _Now_ we're talking!

After Mr. A goes inside, we cross street to see building from other side. At least 20 floors. Penthouse. Roof garden. The works.

**5:40**: Surprise! Mr. A comes back out of building with a DOG.

Note: He walks his own dog?

**5:43**: Dog does his business, and Mr. A scoops it up with a plastic bag.

5:45: Mr. A leaves dog tied around parking meter and goes into pizza place. Orders a slice to go.

5:55: Buys bananas from fruit cart on street. Inspects each one for bruises.

6:00: Mr. A (and dog) go back into apartment building. Surveillance over.

"That's it," Ursula said after Mr. Alexander (and his dog) went back inside. "We must have the wrong guy. That's just *not* big-bucks behavior. He rides the subway, walks his own dog, scoops poop off the sidewalk, eats take-out pizza, buys his own bananas...that's just *not* living in the lap of luxury."

"You think just 'cause he acts like a normal person, he's not rich?" I asked.

"I'm just saying it doesn't *seem* like it," Ursula said. "Everything we saw was totally ordinary."

"He lives in a pretty nice building," I reminded her.

"It wasn't *that* fancy," Ursula argued. "And when you look at all the facts together, he just doesn't seem like the kind of guy who could afford to donate millions of dollars worth of books. He seems like a *thousandaire*, max."

"He could still be rich," I said. "Maybe he just *likes* riding the subway. Maybe he *enjoys* walking his dog. And if you walk your dog, you have to deal with the mess—it's part of the territory."

Ursula didn't look too convinced.

"And *everyone* likes pizza," I added.

Ursula *still* didn't look convinced. And I have to say, I wasn't really believing it myself anymore.

It was getting late, so we decided to start looking for a bus to ride back to our side of town.

"I'm *sure* Kathleen was saying that Mr. Alexander was the book donor," Ursula said as we walked to the bus stop. "And she gave us the address, and we went to that address, and there was a Mr. Alexander there. So how could we have gone wrong?"

"Maybe we *didn't* go wrong," I said, trying to be optimistic again. "Maybe he's just a different kind of gazillionaire."

"Maybe so," Ursula said with her forehead all wrinkly.

It *was* a mystery, all right....

# CHAPTER 9
# HE DID WHAT?

The next morning before school, we told the others about the subway-riding, dog-walking, poop-scooping, pizza-eating, banana-buying "gazillionaire."

They were shocked. Especially about the poop.

"He did *what?*" Anika asked.

HE SCOOPED THE POOP!

"He scooped the poop," Ursula repeated, shaking her head in disbelief.

"Well, maybe he's a real down-to-earth rich person," Anika said. "I'm sure there's such a thing."

"Either that, or somehow we had the wrong guy," Ursula said.

"If we had the wrong guy, then he must've been *really* weirded out by our letter," Anika pointed out.

"But we saw him reading the letter, and he didn't look weirded out, did he, Spencer?" Ursula asked. "He looked kind of happy...and impressed."

Ursula looked very proud when she said the "impressed" part.

"I don't know," I said with a shrug. "Maybe he was just impressed that we made such a big effort, and maybe he was just smiling because it was such a funny mistake."

Ursula glowered.

"I guess we'll see what happens—he has our school's number," Anika said. "Maybe he'll call and say we got the wrong guy."

Everyone looked depressed.

"*Or*—maybe he'll call and say he'll send us our books!" Anika added with a smile.

✳ ✳ ✳ ✳

Later that day, Julian, Ursula, and I were sitting in math class when, to our surprise, Mrs. Spicer came to the door. She walked into the room in her usual tottery way and went straight up to Miss Pryor at the chalkboard.

As she whispered in Miss Pryor's ear, Miss Pryor's eyes immediately met mine. I knew what this was about! Sure enough...

"Ursula, Spencer, and Julian," Miss Pryor said, "Mrs. Spicer needs to speak with you in the hallway."

Julian and Ursula looked at me with excited eyes. We all jumped out of our seats and followed Mrs. Spicer out the door.

"Are we getting our books?" Ursula asked as soon as we were in the hall.

"Yes, we are!" Mrs. Spicer said with a huge smile. "The donor's assistant called, and we're all set—he'll be sending out the books early next week!"

"**YES!**" we all said really loudly.

"Shhh," Mrs. Spicer said. "Let's use our inside voices, please!"

"Does Miss Butt know?" Ursula asked in her inside voice.

"Yes," Mrs. Spicer said. "I already passed along the message to her. She's waiting for you in the library with your friends. I thought we'd all meet down there."

So we all walked S-L-O-W-L-Y down to the library with Mrs. Spicer. The whole time I was marveling over the fact that Mr. Alexander-the-Ordinary really *was* the donor after all. I could tell Ursula was thinking the same thing.

### ✳ ✳ ✳ ✳

When we finally got to the library, we found Blitz and Anika talking excitedly to Miss Butt at one of the tables.

"Did you hear? We're getting our books!" Blitz called to us when we walked in.

"YEAH!" we all said.

"I can't *believe* it," Ursula said.

"Nicely done, you guys!" Miss Butt cheered.

"And we have even *more* good news," Mrs. Spicer said.

"What?" we all asked.

"Mr. Alexander was so impressed with your letter, he's invited you all to his office today after school!"

"He wants to meet US?!" we all said.

"Yes," Mrs. Spicer said. "He really wants to meet the kids who managed to track him down."

We all looked at each other with enormous eyes.

"I'll be coming with you," Miss Butt said.

"And *I'll* call all of your parents to get permission," Mrs. Spicer said, pulling out a piece of paper. "I just need the numbers where I can reach them this afternoon."

It was kind of ridiculous that today we needed *permission* to do the same thing we did yesterday. But whatever. We all waited while Mrs. Spicer wrote down our parents' names and numbers in her perfect swooping handwriting.

"I can't *wait* to see Mr. Alexander's office," Ursula said as we walked back to class. "I bet it'll look really *important.* Then maybe he'll seem more gazillionairish."

We were all so excited, it was hard to even *think* about finishing up the day in school.

## \* \* \* \*

Miss Butt with pink cheeks

When school was finally over, we all met in the library. Miss Butt had put on some makeup, so her cheeks were bright pink. It kind of looked like she had a fever.

We were just about to head out when Mrs. Spicer appeared.

"I just came to wish you bon voyage!" she said excitedly. "I wish I could come, but Mr. Naulty needs my help in the office."

We all tried not to wince when she mentioned *him*.

"I brought you a special snack for the trip," Mrs. Spicer said, holding up a plastic bag. "Barbecued almonds and dried cranberries!"

"Thanks," we all said, wondering how she could've possibly come up with a combination like that.

"I can't wait to hear all about it tomorrow," she said. "Have a good time!"

And so we were off.

# CHAPTER 10
## ALEXANDER THE GREAT

When we got to Mr. Alexander's office building, we found Jelly Donut at the front desk again (but this time minus the donut). He called up to Mr. Alexander to let him know we were here, and then he printed out official visitor badges for us.

Since the badges had our first and last names on them, we found out that Miss Butt's first name is Marcia. Jelly made a real big deal of her last name, which she didn't exactly appreciate.

NOW IS THAT "BUT" AS IN "NO IFS, ANDS, OR BUTS", OR "BUTT" AS IN THE THING I'M SITTING ON?

THE LATTER.

my badge

565 FIFTH AVENUE

Spencer Strange

Floor: 24    Guest of: Jonathan Alexander

Mr. Alexander was waiting for us when we got out of the elevator.

"Hello!" he said cheerfully as we stepped out.

He held out his hand to each of us one by one, and we all introduced ourselves. Mr. Alexander repeated each of our names as he shook our hands and looked at us right in the eye with a big smile. He seemed like a really cool guy.

"I was just *so* impressed when I got your letter," Mr. Alexander said. "I thought, now these kids are *really* resourceful if they figured out how to get my name *and* address. Miss Butt told me that you managed to get the delivery company to tell you. All I can say is, hats off to you."

We all smiled.

"And that letter," Mr. Alexander added, "was extremely professional. Who wrote it?"

Ursula looked like she'd just won an Oscar.

"Me," she said, with a much quieter voice than usual.

Mr. Alexander nodded at her approvingly.

"And that envelope definitely got my attention," he added. "Whose handiwork was that?"

"Mine," Anika said, also with a hushed voice.

"Well, nicely done, all of you," Mr. Alexander said. "Now if you'll all follow me, I'll give you a quick tour of the company."

And so Mr. Alexander walked us into the company, swiping a card that made the double glass doors in front of us slide open.

The first thing we saw was a big shiny sign that said "Silver and Reyes." We stopped there for a second while Mr. Alexander explained that his company was all about investments—you know, stock market stuff. It was too bad, because I was kind of hoping it would be a company that actually made something (besides money), like cars or refrigerators. But anyway.

Inside, there were a lot of people sitting at desks with short walls around them. They were all working on computers or talking on the phone. Not exactly exciting.

At least Ursula was interested. She asked lots of questions.

The best part of the tour was when Mr. Alexander took us to a meeting room where the walls were all made of glass. Then he went inside and pressed a button, and the glass suddenly turned white, so you couldn't see through it anymore.

"For privacy," Mr. Alexander explained.

We were all totally impressed, especially Blitz, who looked like his eyes were about to fall out of his head.

We wanted to try flipping the switch a few times, but suddenly a man came in and looked at Mr. Alexander with a not-so-friendly face.

"I have this room booked at 4:00," he said. "So if you don't mind, I have to set up my presentation."

"Sorry," Mr. Alexander said quickly. "We were just leaving."

And so we quickly left.

I was kind of surprised to see Mr. Alexander get treated like that. After all, he was supposed to be some kind of big shot at this company, so you'd think he'd get more respect. Anika gave me a look that said she was surprised, too.

Anyway, after that, we went up a flight of stairs and walked along a hallway of enormous offices with glass doors. Inside, people were talking, but you couldn't hear a word they were saying. Most of the time, the people didn't even notice us walk past. But there was one lady who smiled and waved from her desk. She looked nice.

"I wonder which office is *his*," Blitz whispered excitedly.

But we didn't go inside *any* of the offices. Instead, Mr. Alexander led the way to a small desk on the opposite side of the hallway. Sitting on the desk were all sorts of little presents for us—hats, pens, key chains, and even little notepads with the company name on them. It was like party favor city.

official company
party favors

"Thanks," we all said.

"And thanks for having us here," Miss Butt added. "It was very kind of you to invite us."

"Certainly," Mr. Alexander said.

"And of course we're also very grateful for the books. That was such a generous thing to do," Miss Butt added.

"I know," Mr. Alexander said, nodding in agreement. "It was a *wonderful* idea."

It was really weird hearing Mr. Alexander compliment himself like that. No one knew what to say, so there was this awkward pause. But that didn't stop Mr. Alexander from jumping right in there and complimenting himself *again*:

"I can't think of a more meaningful gift," he added. "Or a more *important* one."

We all looked at each other in disbelief. Talk about tooting your own horn! This guy was out of control.

Then Mr. Alexander launched into a speech about the importance of books for "today's young people."

While he was talking, my eyes wandered around the desk where we were standing, and, to my surprise, I saw:

# MR. ALEXANDER'S DOG!

So this was *his* desk? What happened to the big office?

I quickly scanned the desk for other clues about Mr. Alexander, and I saw a stack of business cards that read: *Jonathan Alexander, Executive Assistant.*

An executive *assistant*? Weren't gazillionaire types supposed to *have* assistants, not *be* assistants?

And that's when I realized what might be going on here. Maybe Mr. Alexander wasn't the one who donated all the books. Maybe he just worked for the person who did. Maybe *that* was why he was heaping praise on the whole idea. Of course!

So I decided to test out my theory. I had to do it carefully, because I didn't want to offend him if he really *was* the donor.

"So, how did you come up with the idea to donate the books?" I asked.

"*Me?*" Mr. Alexander said. "*I* didn't donate the books."

"YOU *DIDN'T?*" everyone asked all at once.

"I could tell from your letter that's what you thought," Mr. Alexander said. "But I told the woman I spoke with at your school, Mrs...what was her name?"

"SPICER," we all said.

"Yes, her," Mr. Alexander said. "I told her I was just the guy who did all the legwork, ordered the trucks, picked out the books, sent all the letters...but not the person who paid the bill. Didn't she tell you?"

"NO," we all said, thinking of Mrs. Spicer and how excited she was. How could she have forgotten to tell us such an important thing?

"Then who was it?" Ursula asked.

"My boss," Mr. Alexander said.

"Do we get to meet him?" Julian asked.

"Her," Mr. Alexander corrected. "Her name is Annabel Reyes."

"As in Silver and Reyes?" Anika asked with wide eyes.

"Exactly," Mr. Alexander said. "And she's very much looking forward to meeting all of you. She should be ready for us now."

And so we all set down our party favors and walked toward one of the offices down the hall. And that's when I realized it: Ms. Reyes was the woman who smiled at us when we walked past!

Mr. Alexander pulled open the office door and we all stepped inside.

"Hello!" Ms. Reyes said, standing up from her desk. "Welcome!"

WELCOME!

Mr. Alexander introduced all of us by name, and Ms. Reyes shook all of our hands, looking us right in the eye, just like Mr. Alexander did. I have to say, she was very pretty. And her office was really cool. It had a huge window with a view out over the city.

"Thank you very much for the books," Miss Butt said. "That was a wonderful thing to do."

"Oh, I've been wanting to do it for a long time," Ms. Reyes said. "I grew up in the city, you see—I went to public schools—and I've always promised myself that someday I would give back. And last month I decided that 'someday' had come. Fortunately I had Jon's help, or I never could've done it."

We all turned to smile at Mr. Alexander, who smiled and looked down, being modest.

"He really did his homework and picked out some absolutely wonderful books," Ms. Reyes continued. "I had some titles in mind, but he went through catalog after catalog and found the very best books. It was really a huge effort on his part, and he did it all on his own time, as it's not part of his job here at the company."

"Thank you," we all said, looking at Mr. Alexander in a whole new way, now that we finally understood his part in all this.

"It was my pleasure," Mr. Alexander said. "It was for a very important cause. I was very inspired by it, because I've always been a real bookworm, just like Ms. Reyes."

"So *that's* why you decided to give books," Miss Butt said, smiling at Ms. Reyes.

"Exactly," Ms. Reyes said. "I've always loved to read. When I was growing up, I used to tear through books like nobody's business—sometimes I'd even read two or three at the same time. Books were my world."

"I used to be the same way," Miss Butt said.

"My family couldn't afford to buy very many books," Ms. Reyes continued, "and I could only go to the public library if my parents took me. So I was really counting on my school library. And I remember feeling like it just wasn't cutting it."

"I'm afraid our library isn't the greatest, either," Miss Butt said. "It's been needing a major overhaul for a long time. I just don't have much budget to work with, unfortunately."

"Most of the books are older than *we* are," Ursula chimed in.

"*And* they have all kinds of stuff scribbled in them," Julian said. "*Nasty* stuff."

"And the tables have bad stuff carved in them, too," Blitz added.

"I try to erase the writing that's in *pencil*," Miss Butt said, looking flustered.

"I'm sure you do your best," Ms. Reyes said. "I know what you're up against."

Ms. Reyes looked like she was thinking for a moment. Then suddenly she turned and spoke to Mr. Alexander.

"Could you call for a car? A large one?" she asked. "I'd like to ride over to their school and see the library we're talking about. I think we might be able to help a little more."

"Sure," Mr. Alexander said. "I'll be right back."

And Mr. Alexander walked out to make the call. The rest of us—especially Miss Butt—were in total shock. Ms. Reyes was coming to our *school*?

"I'm afraid the library will be a mess," Miss Butt said. "I haven't had a chance to straighten it up today because we came here right after school."

"Don't worry," Ms. Reyes said with a smile. "I'm not going to criticize. I just want to help if I can."

## ✳ ✳ ✳ ✳

We took the elevator down to the lobby with Ms. Reyes and Mr. Alexander, and you know what was waiting outside?

# A LIMO!

We all got inside and spread out on the big cushy seats. Talk about riding in style! It was my first time ever in a limo—same for Ursula, Anika, Blitz, and Julian (but not for Miss Butt, because she rode in one to her high school prom).

The ride to our school was way too short, even though we got the driver to take us on a detour through Times Square so we could see all the lights.

It was too bad none of the kids were at school when we got there, because they would have totally freaked out to see us pull up in a deluxe limo with tinted windows and a driver who opens the door. But what can you do.

After we got out of the limo, we all went straight to the library. Ms. Reyes looked around quietly while Miss Butt apologized for the mess. The rest of us just watched in silence, wondering what Ms. Reyes was thinking. Finally she spoke:

"I think we can spruce this place up, don't you?" she asked Mr. Alexander.

"Absolutely," Mr. Alexander said.

And then Ms. Reyes started giving out instructions that Mr. Alexander jotted down on his clipboard.

We all just stood back and watched, amazed.

WE NEED MORE LIGHT, MORE SHELVES, SOME NICE CARPETING, SOME COMPUTER WORKSTATIONS OVER THERE ... AND SOME COMFORTABLE CHAIRS OVER THERE ... AND LETS SEND IN SOME NEW TABLES AND CHAIRS TO REPLACE THESE.

"Anything else you think you need?" Ms. Reyes asked us when she finished.

"Oh no," Miss Butt said. "This is more than enough already!"

"You're very, very *generous*," Blitz said, looking at Ms. Reyes in awe.

"Yeah," Ursula said. "Most people would keep their money or spend it on themselves."

"I don't enjoy spending money on myself," Ms. Reyes said. "There was a time when I did, but now I just want to share my luck as much as I can."

"Well, we're definitely lucky we met *you*," Anika said.

*That* was for sure.

"And *you*," Anika added, looking at Mr. Alexander.

No doubt about *that*, either.

# CHAPTER 11
## TOTAL MAKEOVER

**O**ver the next few weeks, Mr. Alexander helped us give our library a total makeover. We got new shelves, new chairs, new tables, new lights, new carpeting, and even four new computers with internet connections that actually work. It was a complete transformation!

And, of course, we *also* got our truckload of new books. There were mysteries, spy stories, science fiction, real-life adventures, and tons of other books about sports, cars, airplanes, spaceships—you name it. For the first time, the shelves of the M.S. 1024 library were filled with books I'd actually check out.

Just like before, Ms. Reyes didn't want any credit for the library makeover (she says she's a very private person). But still, Anika thought we should send a thank-you note, so she made a giant one, and everyone at school signed it. They were all totally thrilled with the new library.

All the teachers and staff were really excited, too, especially Miss Butt.

And Mrs. Spicer.

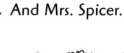

And even Mr. Naulty was impressed.

We made sure Mr. Naulty knew that *we'd* made it happen, since he was the one who told us that there was nothing we could do.

"See, Mr. Naulty, we got the books and *then* some!" Ursula said when Mr. Naulty came to see the finished library.

"Indeed," Mr. Naulty said, looking around.

"The moral of the story is, you should *always* read your mail," Ursula said.

Mr. Naulty looked at her with his big eyebrows stitched together.

"What do you mean?" he asked.

"In case other donation offers come along," Anika said quickly, since we didn't want Mr. Naulty to know that Mrs. Spicer had told us how he'd never bothered to read the letters from Mr. Alexander. That would've definitely gotten Mrs. Spicer in trouble.

"This was a very lucky thing," Mr. Naulty said. "I doubt anything like it will ever come along again."

"Well, instead of *waiting* for something good to come along, maybe we can *make* something good happen again," Anika suggested.

"That would be nice," Mr. Naulty nodded, his eyebrows still stitched together. Then he turned around and ducked out the door. You could tell he was really uncomfortable. It was actually kind of funny.

**\* \* \* \***

In other good news, Blitz built a new voice changer, and it's *way* better than the first one. It has *four* voices this time, not just the tough-guy voice.

It was really cool to try it out. And *now* we don't have to feel bad anymore about the old voice changer going the way of the black hole. It was all in the name of progress.

So, anyway, that's about it for this operation. I think this one got pretty amazing results—I mean, how often does spy work get you a completely made-over library? Not bad for a few weeks worth of espionage!

Until next time,

*Spencer*

P.S. Oh, I forgot to mention: Ursula finally figured out her "rock, paper, scissors" problem. For *now*, at least.

# Spy Gear Manual
## Voice Changer

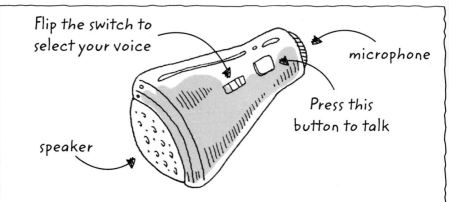

Flip the switch to select your voice

microphone

Press this button to talk

speaker

## Sound Check!

What can you do to get the best sound out of your voice changer? Try some experiments to find out:

1. What happens if you talk softly?

2. What happens if you talk really loud?

3. What happens if you talk a little higher (squeakier) or a little lower (deeper) than your normal voice? How does that change the way each voice sounds?

### Blitz's Tech Report

When you speak into the microphone, the microchip inside the voice changer converts the sound into electronic signals, then changes the signals, then converts them back into sound that comes out of the speaker.

## Voice Choice

With a friend as your audience, try all four voices on the voice changer, saying the same thing each time. Have your friend listen to you speak and rank the voices on the chart below. Rank <u>your</u> favorites, too!

| Voice # | Sounds coolest | Sounds clearest |
|---|---|---|
| 1. Squeaky | | |
| 2. Robotic | | |
| 3. Scary | | |
| 4. Booming | | |

## Voice Change Challenge #1

Gather together a group of friends. Turn your back (or close your eyes) and take a few steps away from your friends. Then ask your friends to choose one person to use the voice changer to speak to you. Your friend should say something simple (like "Hello, how are you?"), using any one of the voice settings.

Can you figure out which friend is speaking to you, or is your friend's voice so different that you can't tell who's speaking?

CAN YOU TELL WHO I AM?

# Voice Change Challenge #2

Test how well your voice changer gets your message across. Say something using one of the voice settings, and ask a group of friends to write down what they think you said. Then switch settings and say something else. Do the same thing for each one of the voice settings.

Then look at what your friends wrote down. Which voice got your message across to the most people? Which voice was the hardest for your friends to understand?

**Talking Tip**
To get the best results, speak slowly and pronounce each word clearly.

MEET ME AT MY PLACE AFTER SCHOOL.

Until our next operation,
—Spencer

ENJOY ALL YOUR VOICE CHOICES!